Journey to Dragon Mountain

adapted by Natalie Shaw
based on the screenplay written by Marc Seal

Simon Spotlight
New York London Toronto Sydney New Delhi

SIMON SPOTLIGHT
An imprint of Simon & Schuster Children's Publishing Division
1230 Avenue of the Americas, New York, New York 10020
© 2014 HIT (MTK) Limited. Mike the Knight™ and logo and Be a Knight, Do It Right™
are trademarks of HIT (MTK) Limited. Nickelodeon and all related titles and logos
are trademarks of Viacom International Inc. All rights reserved, including the right of
reproduction in whole or in part in any form. SIMON SPOTLIGHT and colophon are
registered trademarks of Simon & Schuster, Inc. For information about special discounts
for bulk purchases, please contact Simon & Schuster Special Sales at 1-866-506-1949 or
business@simonandschuster.com.
Manufactured in the United States of America 0814 LAK
10 9 8 7 6 5 4 3 2
ISBN 978-1-4814-1989-5
ISBN 978-1-4814-1990-1 (eBook)

The town is very peaceful today.
Everyone's having fun as they play.
Run, ride, frolic, or sing, skip, and shout.
There's nothing at all to be worried about!

Mike the Knight and his sister, Evie, were playing outside by the hay cart.

"I wish we could have a *real* adventure!" Mike told his sister. Just then they heard a loud noise. They leapt out of the way just in time—before two objects crashed into the hay cart.

It was their father, the King, and his horse, Guinevere!
"Oh, Dad, we've missed you so much!" Mike said. "But
where did you and Guinevere come from? You *fell* out of the
sky!"

"Well," said the King, "it's actually a good story."
All of Glendragon gathered around. The King said that
he and his horse were exploring faraway lands when they
discovered a strange mountain—a mountain that glowed and
sparkled at night.

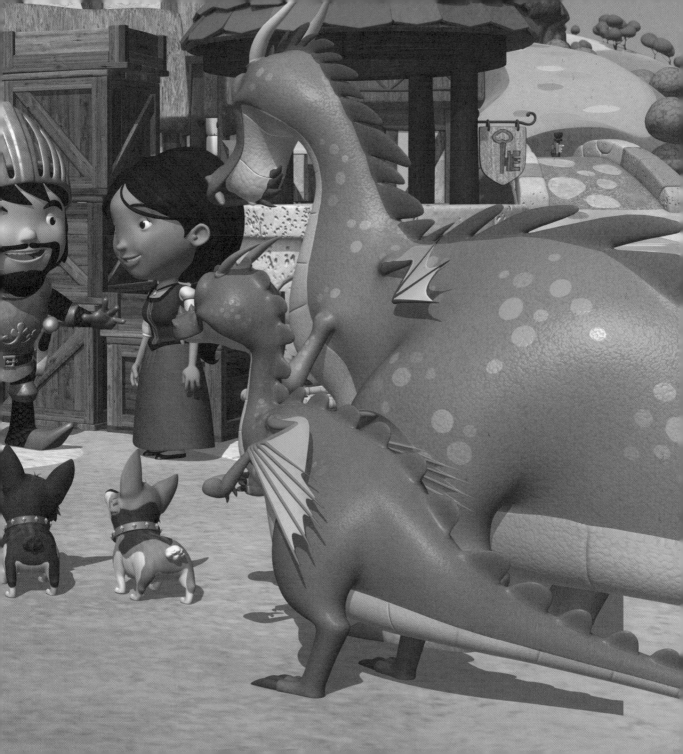

"The people in the land called it Dragon Mountain," the Kin said. "They said a giant dragon lived inside, guarding a huge crystal jewel! When I arrived, Vikings had just taken the jewel, thinking it was a shiny toy. I rescued the jewel from the Viking and climbed up the mountain to return it to the dragon."

"But before I
could find the dragon, the
dragon found me!" continued the
King. "It must have thought that *I* had taken
the jewel! It picked me and Guinevere up, flew us
to Glendragon, and dropped us in the hay cart!"
The King assured the villagers that Glendragon was
afe as long as the dragon had its crystal. He then returned to
he castle with the Queen and Evie.

Mike, Sparkie, and Squirt walked to the castle too, but Squirt followed behind the others. He was still scared of the big dragon. That's when a giant crystal fell from the sky and landed by his feet! Before Squirt could do anything, three Vikings grabbed the crystal and used it to play catch!

Squirt caught up with Mike and
parkie and told them what he had seen.
Mike!" Squirt said, panting. "The Vikings
ave the crystal jewel again!"
"We have to tell Dad!" Mike exclaimed.

When Mike arrived at the castle, the King had already heard the news from the villagers.

"Don't be alarmed," Mike's father cried out. "I am your King and my mission is to rescue the crystal jewel, take it back to Dragon Mountain, and make Glendragon safe again!"

Mike jumped up and added, "And my name is Mike the Knight, and my mission is to rescue the crystal jewel with my father!"

"I'm sorry, Mike," said the King, "but it is just too dangerous. Your mission is to stay here and look after the Queen and Evie."

"Aw, but Dad!" Mike protested. "I've learned so many knightly skills since you've been away! I'm ready to go on a *rea* knightly mission with you!"

"And I want to help too, with my magic," added Evie.

But their father refused. He mounted his horse, and left on his mission.

When everyone left the courtyard, Mike decided that he would follow his father and show him that he had learned to be very knightly! So he put on his armor and drew his enchanted sword. But instead of a sword, it was . . .

"A picture of Dad?" Mike asked. "It's great—but how's it going to help?"

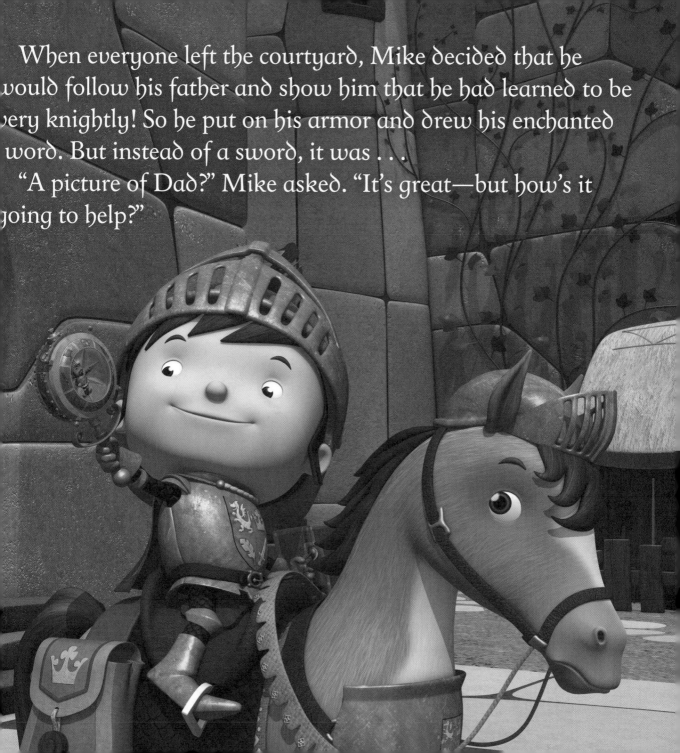

Mike followed the King to the beach. He saw the King trying
to get the crystal away from the Vikings, without much luck.
That's when the King discovered that Mike—and Evie, too—
had followed him there, hoping to help with the mission.

Together, they got the crystal from the Vikings.
"You shouldn't have followed me," the King told Mike and Evie.
"But now that you're here, let's tackle this mission as a family!"
"Team Family Glendragon!" they all shouted.
"Come on, then, you two," the King announced. "Off to Dragon
Mountain to give back the crystal jewel!"

Together, Team Family Glendragon walked for what seemed like ages.

"Look! There it is!" Mike said as they finally saw Dragon Mountain towering before them.

When they reached the mountain, they climbed on foot until

"Mike and Evie, you both stay here," the King said. "I want you to wait here while I return the crystal to the dragon."

As soon as the King entered the cave, Mike and Evie saw the shadow of a giant dragon follow quickly behind him.

"We have to save him from the giant dragon!" Evie told Mike. "I know he told us not to, but . . ."

. . . but it's time to be a knight who do it right!" Mike doded.

That's when Mike realized that the picture on the edge of his sword was actually a compass. It led them straight to the King. But just as they were reunited, the King fell into a ravine!

With a little help from Mike's knightly training, Evie and Mike rescued their father.

"Mike, that was the fastest knightly thinking I've ever seen. What a great knight you are!" the King told Mike.

Together, they gave the crystal to the giant dragon. They were surprised to see Sparkie and Squirt were there too. They had followed behind Evie, Mike, and the King. They wanted to help save Glendragon from the giant dragon, even though Squirt was scared.

But they found out that the giant dragon wasn't scary after all. It was Squirt's father!

"Squirt wandered off when we were moving here to Dragon Mountain," the giant dragon told the King. "His mother and I thought we'd *never* find him again."

Squirt's father placed the crystal in a nest at the center
f the cave, and the most amazing thing happened. The jewel
racked open to reveal a baby dragon! The jewel wasn't a jewel
fter all: It was an *egg*!

Everyone returned to Glendragon much happier than when they had left. Squirt was reunited with his family—and a new baby sister. And Mike and Evie had gone on their first mission with the King.

"There's nothing we can't do together!" Mike said as everyone cheered. "Team Family Glendragon saved the day!"